For: Vicki, Lily, Edward and Tilly

Rockpool Children's Books
15 North Street
Marton
Warwickshire
CV23 9RJ

First published in Great Britain by Rockpool Children's Books Ltd. 2007
Text and Illustrations copyright © Stuart Trotter 2007
Stuart Trotter has asserted the moral rights
to be identified as the author and illustrator of this book.

ISBN 0-9553022-5-0
ISBN 978-0-9553022-5-1

A CIP catalogue record of this book is available
from the British Library.

Printed in China

rockpool
children's books

The princess who couldn't sleep.

Stuart Trotter

Up the long, long stairs to bed...

...the little princess lay down her
not-so-sleepy head and said,
"I just can't get to sleep." So...

...she told the butler

...who told the maid

...who told the cook

...who told the housekeeper

...who told the
lady-in-waiting

...who told the queen.
"Ma'am, the princess, she cannot sleep."

Rising from the royal bed,
the queen went to see
the little princess.

"Mummy, I can't get to sleep,"
said the little princess.
"Can I have a..."

"...a glass of milk? Good idea," purred the queen. So...

...in came the royal cow, which was milked by the royal herdsman.

The little princess sipped
the royal milk. "Yuk!" she spluttered.
"Mummy, all I want is a..."

"...bedtime story? Good idea."
chirped the queen. So...

...in came the royal storyteller, who read
a sleepy story to the little princess.
"Once upon a time," he droned.

The royal cow, the royal herdsman, the
queen - but definitely not
the little princess - all fell fast asleep!
The little princess
prodded the snoring queen.
"Mummy, just a little..."

"...lullaby?
Good idea,"
trilled
the queen.

...in came the royal minstrel, who sang
a soothing song that woke up the royal cow,
the royal herdsman...

...and also most of the palace!

"Sleepy?" asked the queen.
"Not a bit," said the little princess.
"Mummy, all I want is..."

"...to count some sheep?
Good idea,"
bleated the queen.
So...

...in came the royal flock of sheep.

nine, two-ty four, three-ty six...

They proceeded
to jump over
the little princess,

who couldn't count.
So that didn't work.
"Yes?" asked the queen.
"No," said the little princess.

"I know," said the queen.
"A ride in the car."
So...

...the chauffeur, the little princess, the queen, the cow, the royal herdsman, the storyteller, the minstrel, the shepherd, and the sheep, all climbed into the car and went for a gentle ride.

"Dozy?" asked the queen.
"Not a bit,"
said the little princess.
"What I really need is a..."

"...cuddle!"
said the little princess,
finally.
"Oh," said the queen.
"Is that all?"

So, the queen
dismissed the cow,
the herdsman,
the storyteller,
the minstrel,
the shepherd , the sheep,
the chauffeur and the car,
gave the little princess
a cuddle and...

...they both fell fast asleep. Until...

..."Mummy, I can't get to sleep!"
bellowed the little prince.